This book belongs to:

iva Rose

PNI

Lyndon Mcu PRimny Shoo

First published 2012 by Walker Books Ltd
87 Vauxhall Walk, London SE11 5HJ

2 4 6 8 10 9 7 5 3 1

© 2012 Lucy Cousins
Lucy Cousins font © 2012 Lucy Cousins

The author/illustrator has asserted her moral rights

Illustrated in the style of Lucy Cousins by King Rollo Films Ltd

Maisy™. Maisy is a registered trademark of Walker Books Ltd, London

Printed in China

British Library Cataloguing in Publication Data:
a catalogue record for this book is
available from the British Library.

ISBN 978-1-4063-3745-7

www.walker.co.uk

Maisy Goes on a Sleepover

Lucy Cousins

WALKER BOOKS
AND SUBSIDIARIES
LONDON · BOSTON · SYDNEY · AUCKLAND

Tallulah gave Maisy a letter at the playground. It was an invitation to a sleepover.

Maisy accepted at once, even though she had never been on a sleepover before.

Maisy started packing. She would need lots of things. Pyjamas, toothbrush, a sleeping bag, clean clothes for the morning. What else? Panda would come, too. Ooh! How exciting!

Maisy and Panda
went to Tallulah's house.

"Welcome," Tallulah said.
"Come inside and meet
my new friend, Ella."

Maisy and Panda liked Ella straightaway. Ella had been on a sleepover before and she wasn't shy at all.

They played together and everyone talked and talked about all sorts of things.

Tallulah put on some music,

and Ella did a dance,

which made
everyone laugh.

So then they all tried it.
They called it
Ella's Wriggle
and Roll.

Now it was time for Tallulah's special sleepover supper.

There were sandwiches, cupcakes, fruit and ice cream to finish. Ooh! It was delicious!

Afterwards they played games –
skipping and chasing,

hide-and-seek
    and exploring.

It was strange getting ready
for bed in Tallulah's house.
They snuggled all the
bedding up close together.

Ella made them laugh again by bouncing on the bed.

They put
on their
night
clothes,

and went to
the bathroom
one after
the other.

Maisy read everyone a bedtime story, but no one went to sleep. They kept on laughing and talking for ages.

Maisy told Panda she thought sleepovers were really good fun and perhaps next time she would invite everyone to her house.

At last, everyone
fell asleep. Goodnight,
Maisy. Goodnight, Panda.
Goodnight, everyone!
Sweet dreams...

See you in the morning!